Contemplations of the Faithful

J. Clark

As such I must acknowledge first the Lord, God, Messiah, Jesus…however you call upon Him I must give glory and credit for allowing someone as myself the honor and task of writing this collection. Afterwards I acknowledge my family and loved ones. Without your love and support where would one be doing? Love always matters. Surround yourself in it.

Times are hard. The world is harsh. We should realize that each day is precious and should make them count.

A psalm is defined as "a sacred song or hymn, in particular any of those in the biblical Book of Psalms and used in Christian and Jewish worship". In the Bible there are 150 psalms that are attributed to be written by King David praising, worshipping, and pouring out to God. In such a fashion, *Contemplations of the Faithful* aims to pour out to God life through the eyes of those in the 18-35 age range.

This chapbook came from an idea, a whisper to write poem after poem respectfully and honestly. This sounds like an easy feat, but it proves to be more complicated than I realized. It is a collection of personal experiences and many different interactions all filtered through the eyes of a single person trying to capture larger than life experiences. Some poems question the human purpose, others the concepts of faith, gender, being overwhelmed by life, suffering, temptation, relations between men and women, and the overall state of the human condition. There will be thirty poems in this first collection.

As you read each separate poem, I do not intend to compare *Contemplations of the Faithful* to the biblical Book of Psalms in any way. Rather if these pages spark your interest in reading the Bible then the objective has been fulfilled.

As always, read on and catch updates on writing and more @writingjclark.

1

O Lord, my God

To give me a gift at a time when reading is no longer leisure.

O why my God?

To scribe words with no audience

Is happening madness in his den.

Drones and media fame have replaced

Story-weavers and scribe-gatekeepers.

Even mere facts are nothing more than circus entertainment.

Is my arrival years too late?

I find solace in words yet others

Lose reality in the media craze.

I lift my heard to see hovering cameras

And a small few know your Son's name.

2

We label people as illegal

Forcing violence on them, then blood

And we justify it---

By separating them by our laws.

3

Blessed are the ones who have a mustard seed of faith.

O Lord, blessed are the ones who don't give in to their sinful fate.

We are blessed even when we don't feel it.

To be alive yes but even more blessed is to thrive.

Smile, give thanks, and rejoice as His children we are unique.

So will our blessings be unique according to His grace and mercy.

On each He give unique favor.

4

Ye of strong heart and soft flesh

Ye of flowing estrogen and bearer of breasts

As the Lord made Eve, He crafted her of bone and clay

And woman walked the Earth.

What is feminine in the age of neutrality?

And how to help when the lead could be missing?

God you created me a woman

But at times I wonder why

As I see my gender struggle with our hearts, minds, relationships…

God I am a woman

But in this era, I wonder why.

5

You do not put more on us than we can bear.

But what we tolerate is so much at times

Yet even that weight feels so small.

We strive to make our flesh mighty but we are so weak through it all.

We long for Your perfection as this is the fight of the creation

Longing to be the Creator.

6

Child do not be anxious for I am always near.

The blur of modern life overtakes us all the time.

I look to the hills

Is this worth it?

The mad rush for wealth, resources in an era

I have no say to be in.

Always busy, always moving, always…

So much stress

A crisis will eventually happen.

Mid-life, quarter-life, eighth-life

More and more keep coming.

I look to the hills and be still.

Help is on the way?

To do the will of the Father,

Believe in the one He sent.

The first step boils down to belief.

Believe in Who you cannot see.

Believe in your evil sin so that you can be saved.

Believe in the Son, the one that the Father sent.

To walk blindly on the freeway is a fault.

To believe without sight is no small task nor for the weak.

Terrifying is it not?

To hope but never know.

To believe but not even see.

To walk without knowing the road.

To try but not succeed?

8

In looking towards the coming future

Do not forget to be thankful for the moment, like now.

9

Every day a beat

Every hour a breath

Every minute a blink

Every second a blessing we get but do not deserve.

Every life is a story unfolding to us

But already known to the Creator.

Everybody significant in such a vast creation we call the universe.

Every year a notch of human progress as we search for the cure

To the condition we call mortality.

10

Be there for your fellow man.

Listen to their burdens and comfort their broken soul.

Pass along the advice of the sages.

If you cannot find a source of plentiful wisdom and take them to them.

Have compassion in your ears and sternness in your heart.

As always, consider each word with love

And act accordingly to the agape love

Of our Creator.

11

Be grateful in suffering, be grateful in thriving

Be grateful for all things for everything works

For the good of those who love Him.

If you do not love Him, *should* you suffer?

Rather, do you deserve to suffer for not loving Him?

12

Longing for sensation

We battle for wealth, love, possessions

We fight for the ability to <u>feel</u>.

Experience sensation to fill our hearts, minds, souls

We live to feel.

We feel to live.

We live to feel free, to shape this world as we please.

To create our lives

Creating our own sensation.

13

He needs to be strong, wealthy, generous, and handsome.

To be 6'5 full of muscular goodness, no belly fat.

A three-car minimum with a four-bedroom house.

Have no kids or wives or alimony—no strings attached.

Must be hella fine like Adonis on Earth

And he must be equipped just right:

Not too long or short, not too skinny or thick

The perfect man for every woman

Many expectations yet not enough reality

For all women on Earth.

14

How expensive is your happiness?

How many sleepless nights must you make change for?

How much stress can your bank bear?

Does your fairy tale end cost the destruction of a marriage?

The pain of star-crossed lovers is a sin?

Swiping money from Peter to buy from Paul?

Even your own soul?

What is the price of your dream in a nightmare world?

Most of all,

Will you be able to pay the price?

15

Tears

Falling down

Hitting the floor

As he walks out

The door to his wife

It breaks your heart

The weekend over

Phone rings

Another

Is coming

Over to you

Wipe away your tears

Five star dinner right now

Kisses, chocolate, hugs, love

All for you

Another Lover

Polyamory.

16

Stranger things than accepted mass shootings

Getting guns without learning to shoot while

Waiting for those chip implants.

Able to travel around the world without leaving the house.

To define your existence in so many syllables nobody can pronounce.

Today is a strange time, a scary time, an exciting time.

A time of change so rapid the human mind boggles to keep pace.

Just what will we do next?

17

Giving praises and honor is a test

When the life you're living isn't the best.

You strive to go above the rest

For greatness I want to nest

The longing to taste of success.

What must we do for you

This generation to be blessed?

We are alive! We can be a mess,

We inherited this world from

Our parents distressed.

Never to be average we must best the test.

18

Not all trends are good.

Male animals work to impress the females.

Dance, battle, skill, action must take place for the right to mate.

How did humans go wrong?

Women out here laboring while males boast on their "ride or die";

Holding up going "50/50" as a way of life,

Still putting traditional labor on her overfull plate.

Males just stopped trying to be in the lead

Failing behind in skills, education, and general drive.

Instead grooming women to accept pathetic as a new norm mobilizing on the Web.

A shifting of performable roles.

19

A blow to the pride as

You walk one way and

Speak on another struggling to

Align word and action in a

World that favors trickery and

Rewards a bleeding heart with poverty.

You want to do one thing yet

Forced to step into another

Life to give the ones you love a

Chance to shine knowing they

Will make the same choice

One day.

20

Day after day my pen is still.

I gaze through grey and see no color.

A cup of sadness with a splash of fatigue to the dough of writing

And you have a hot writer's block pie.

Enjoy with a cold glass of cynicism for the best flavor.

A meal fit for depression.

I should cultivate my God given gift…

Yet this meal demands to be eaten.

Anyone want a slice?

21

O Spring!

Welcome sundresses and shorts

As you say goodbye to overcoats and sweaters.

Melanin ready to absorb the warm rays,

Glowing with the sun.

Booties and sandals and heels all commune at the table of light.

Loose afros and juicy braids fill the skyline of beauty.

We welcome Spring and skin after grueling winter days.

22

Every time I pass by I stop.

Slides up my spine and whispers in my ear,

"Come look."

Tendrils caress my arm with a gentle touch

I know it isn't healthy

But I need this small gratification.

I look.

Bindings full of herbs, tarots, colors, numbers, symbols…

And other too many to count.

My blood says to open and learn ancient words.

Wield the potential inside

I brush against the covers…

…yet eventually

I walk away.

23

I scrub away

Turning brown into red

And can still smell

The stench of failure.

24

The small touch as lovers pass one another

So small yet it screams so loud

As your eyes catch the action in a room of strangers

The pang in your chest is an odd visitor

Of emotion long buried

In the graveyard beating in your chest.

Such a nuisance they are.

Broadcasting love like a light up billboard

Not living in the shadows like the rest of us.

Some poems make you feel good or marvel at the strength of the human soul.

This is not one of those poems.

The ants of anxiety in the skin as she comes close

Buckets rushing down your palms in violent surges,

As the death dealer breaths down your neck.

The horror as the genes you dread are written on your face

Some poems make you feel good or marvel at the strength of the human soul.

This is not one of those poems.

This is the trauma of perfection.

The trauma of perfection as it constricts a living soul.

26

How can we value wisdom yet shun the source?

How can we value love yet make profit off people's pain?

How can actual humans live a life so inhumane?

After all is this the best you can do?

Sleep eludes this jaded soul.

Doctorate potential, middle school results. I would say this is a failure.

Plugging my ears never silences the voice.

You are not satisfied with average. Never will be. Not with average. Stop pretending.

Insanity is kinder than this.

Reach out to the heavens! You want it all---not if you only take it.

What is left? Prayer? Meditation?

Stop being so soft-hearted. Meekness gets you nothing but despair.

It eats away until you cannot scream. A slow acid death.

Take what you deserve!

Can ambition become a sin?

Are you weak? Must be. Just so weak…

As time passes the voice gradually fades. Bit by bit it fades.

Is this humble life worth my constant visits? You can do better. You will never forget.

It's dulled enough to rest. Sleep. A moment of peace…

28

Wires and volts plugged straight

In the mind as we drift

Into a wired reality where we live

Out impossible fantasies flickering

In our eyes as our bodies

Collect dust on the waste side.

Will God hear our cries translated

Into binary?

Sacrifice our souls for digital

Immortality.

Spiritual

To see without seeing, to

Be while being gazing into

The second realm most think nothing

Of day after day

Can everyone truly tap into this?

Is it more like driving

In full fog trying not to

Hit the innocent?

We talk about it

Can you define it, really?

Understand what you have experienced

Without using language to diminish

Such an experience?

Keep it pure with taint?

30

Hand out, reaching so far fingers

Brush next to but not

Enough to grab and your senses

Trip into panic as you struggle

Yet cannot reach

Cannot hold

This feeling multiplied

Thousand upon thousand

Upon thousand in a single

Exhale.

Walking in circles lost

In a desert as dry

As a world

Without compassion.

Made in the USA
Columbia, SC
29 September 2020